Victor Halfwit

THOMAS BERNHARD

Victor Halfwit

TRANSLATED BY MARTIN CHALMERS

ILLUSTRATED BY SUNANDINI BANERJEE

Seagull
BOOKS

LONDON NEW YORK CALCUTTA

Last night,

this is what you have to picture.

These masks, above, which split film in new camera either vertically or horizontally, are used to make trick double exposure shots like the one at right

FREAK MOVIES
Easy with New Amateur Camera

A NEW sixteen-millimeter movie camera now places the professional's bag of tricks in the hands of the amateur.

Fade-outs, double exposures, animations, and enlarged close-ups are only a few of the unusual shots that can be obtained merely by pressing buttons.

Besides lens turret and slow-motion shutter, this new product of the Eastman Kodak laboratories in Rochester, N. Y., has a number of other improvements not found on the ordinary high-grade home movie camera. A crank that runs the film through the camera backwards, an accurate, geared film footage indicator, a unique focusing device, and a shutter that can be opened or closed while the camera is operating are important features.

Lap dissolves, the professional trick of fading one scene into another, are accomplished by means of the simple back-cranking arrangement and special shutter. At the end of a scene, the footage indicator reading is noted and the shutter is closed. Then the film is back-cranked for the footage indicated by the indicator, and when pressed to start the filming of a second scene and the shutter opened slowly. As the light from the first scene is diminished, the light from the second is increased, making the first scene dissolve slowly into the second.

Freak double-exposure stunts are made possible by the masks that slip into a slot at the front of the new camera. The masks come in pairs to split the picture either horizontally or vertically.

By using the vertical masks and manipulating the back crank and shutter, objects and human beings can be materialized realistically from thin air. Ghostly figures can be made to appear, spooks to solidify into real flesh-and-blood men, and the same man shown sitting in several chairs in the same room at the same time.

Dolls and other toys can be brought to life with the animator button on the camera. Each time the button is pressed, a single frame of the film is exposed. By moving the arms and legs of a doll a trifle between each exposure, life-like action can be obtained. When the row of single exposures is projected at the normal speed, the doll will walk, run, jump, or turn graceful somersaults.

A unique focusing device, consisting of a tiny prism that can be raised into place between the lens and the film, increases the accuracy of double exposures made with the new camera. This prism reflects upward against a ground glass mounted at the front of the camera under a magnifying glass the image formed by the lens. Anything that appears on the ground glass will be reproduced in the same position on the film even when the object is but a few inches from the lens. This makes accurate focusing simple.

As a safeguard, the reflecting prism is so arranged that it automatically drops back from its position between the lens and the film the moment the picture-taking button is pressed.

Although other amateur movie cameras have speed ranges that vary from eight to sixty-four frames a second, the new camera is so designed that the speed can

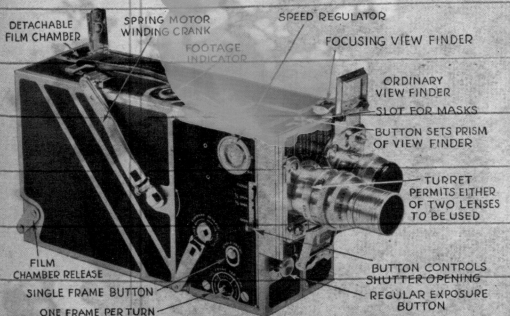

DETACHABLE FILM CHAMBER

SPRING MOTOR WINDING CRANK

FOOTAGE INDICATOR

SPEED REGULATOR

FOCUSING VIEW FINDER

ORDINARY VIEW FINDER

SLOT FOR MASKS

BUTTON SETS PRISM OF VIEW FINDER

TURRET PERMITS EITHER OF TWO LENSES TO BE USED

FILM CHAMBER RELEASE

SINGLE FRAME BUTTON

ONE FRAME PER TURN

BUTTON CONTROLS SHUTTER OPENING

REGULAR EXPOSURE BUTTON

On my way

through the high forest

I stumbled over a man called Victor Halfwit

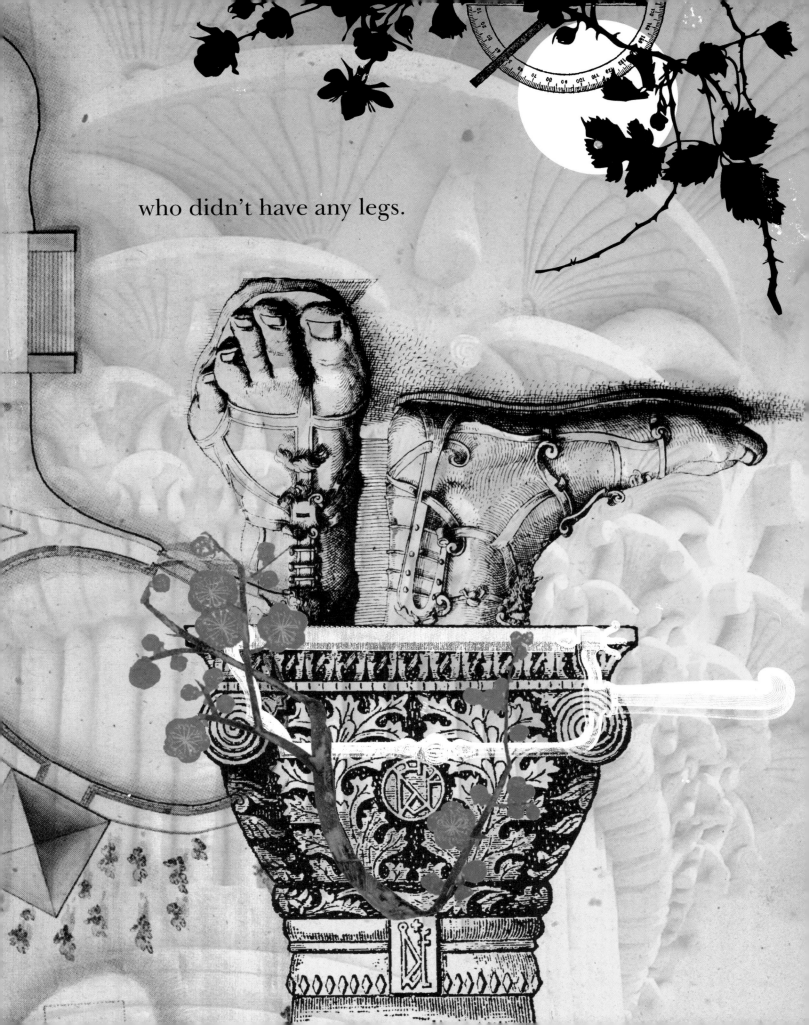

who didn't have any legs.

What is more,
I was very much in a hurry yesterday

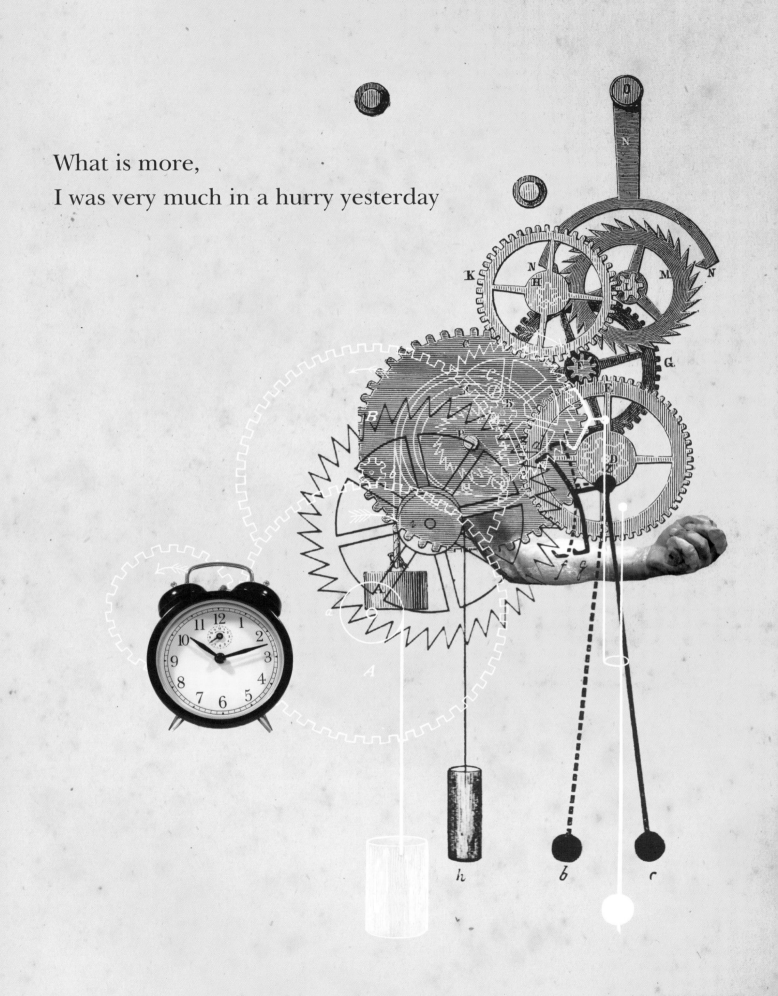

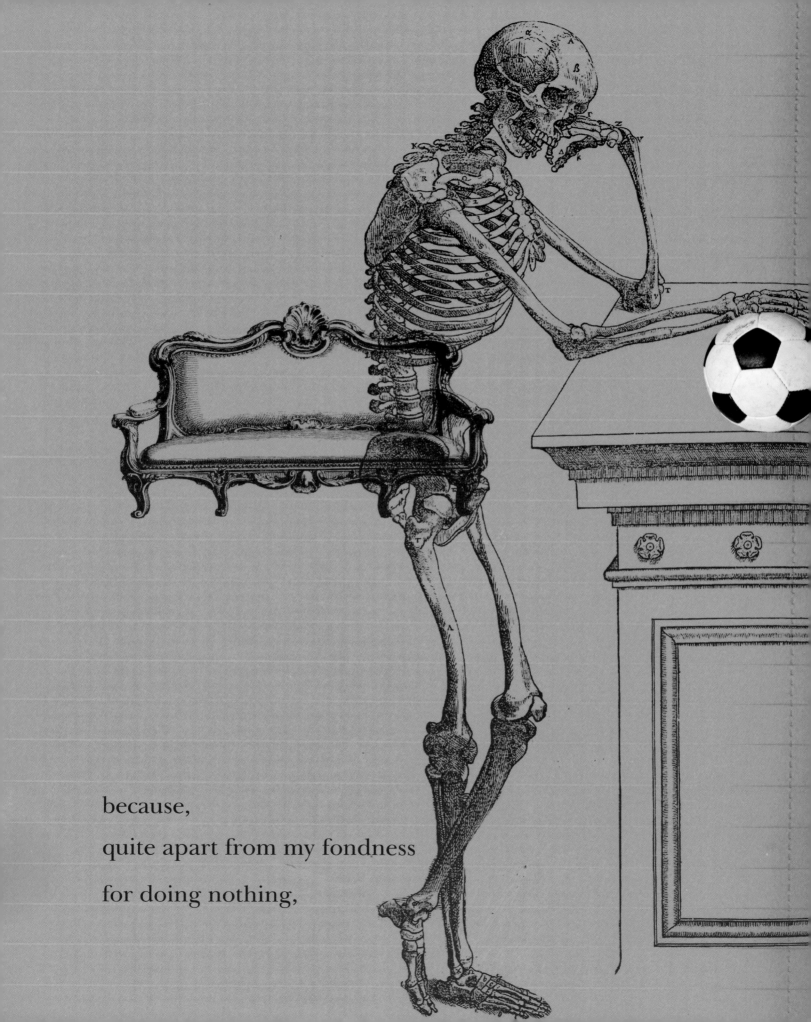

because,

quite apart from my fondness

for doing nothing,

A healthy man on one side of the high forest, in Traich, had called me out to a sick man, a relative of his, on the other side of the high forest, in Föding.

Description of the bones of the head.

1. The frontal bone.
2. The left parietal bone.
3. The temporal bone.
4. The occipital bone.
5. The holes of the orbit where are fixed the eyes.
6. The proper bone of the nose called the nasal.
7. The Zygomatic bone.
8. The maxillary bone.
9. The Teeth.
10. The lower jaw bone.

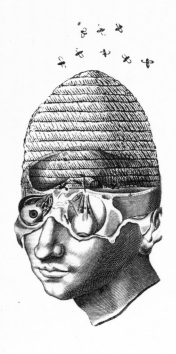

This relative had suddenly fallen victim
to an ailment of the head,

the terrible effects of which
are recorded in the medical books

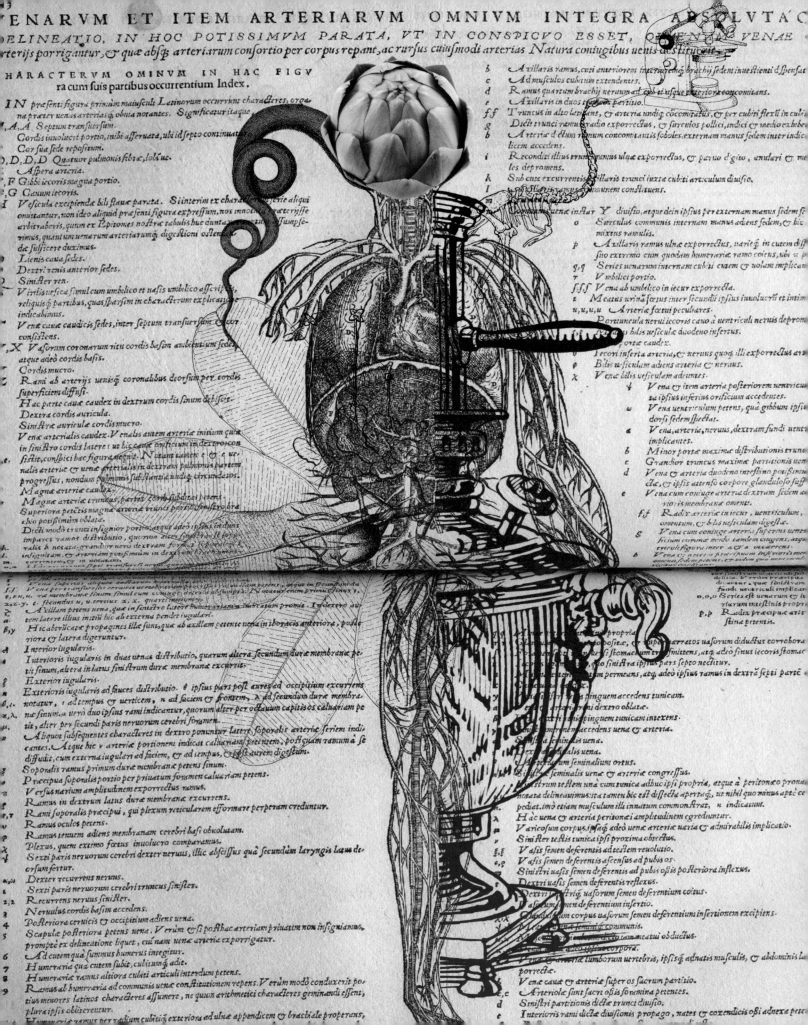

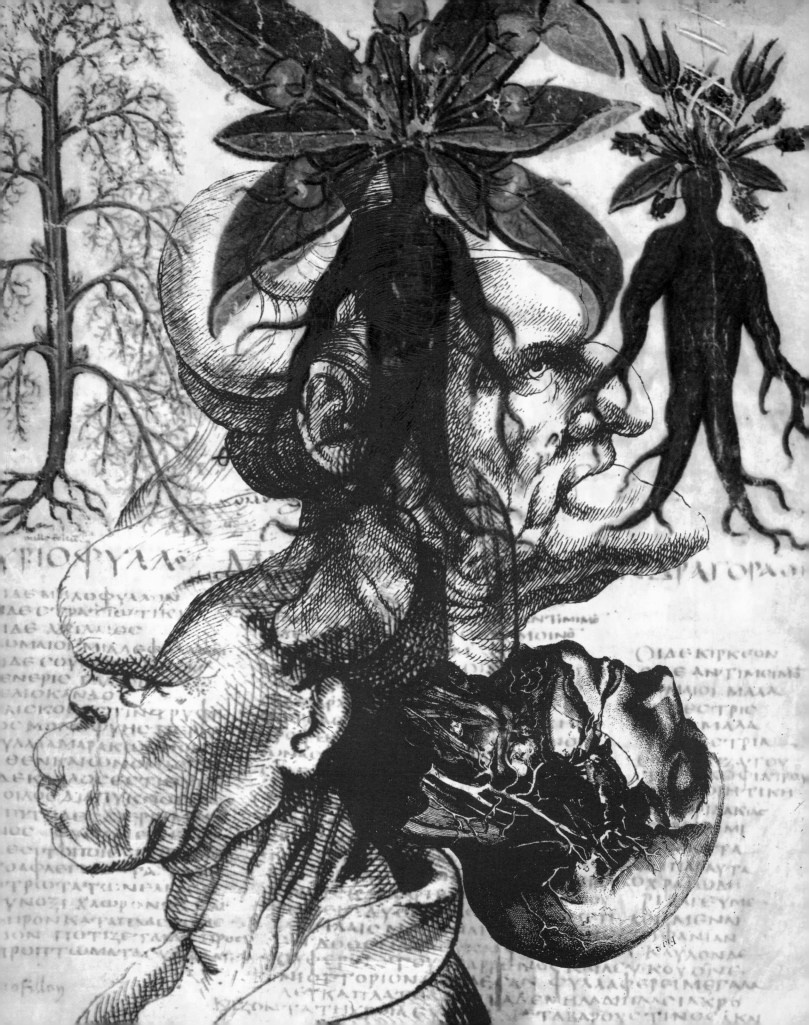

but whose causes no man can explain.

In short, I wanted to walk to the patient

through the high forest, through the deep snow,
that is, employing my best wading-in-the-snow skills,

only to suddenly,
and, as may be imagined, with a start,

AaBbCcDdEeGgHhIiJjK
MmNnOoPpQqRrSsT

ETHELM ROMAN 36 POINT DIDOT

I stumbled over Victor Halfwit in the middle of the high forest.

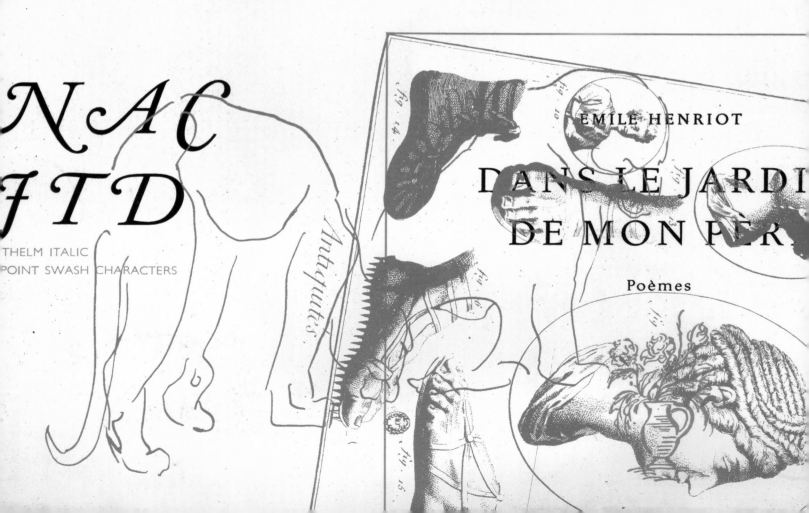

NAC
JTD

THELM ITALIC
POINT SWASH CHARACTERS

EMILE HENRIOT

DANS LE JARDI
DE MON PÈR

Poèmes

'Victor Halfwit'
is how the man, over whom I had stumbled,
and whom I had never before seen,
introduced himself.

IDENTITY CARD

'The locomotive tore them from my body!'
he exclaimed at the very moment when I discovered
that he didn't have any legs,

and in such a way
as if the accident had just happened
to the unfortunate man.

But then it occurred to me

that no train went through the high forest,
that there was no railway track through the high forest,

and nor had I heard any cries,

nothing human,

and, 'of course,' said Victor Halfwit,
'it's already eight years since the accident!'

He was lying in the middle of the high forest,
in the middle of the road, because both his legs,
his wooden legs—

'perhaps because for once I tried to walk faster than usual,' said Victor Halfwit—had suddenly broken.

'All at once I forgot that I have wooden legs, none of my own. I thought that I had my own legs again!'

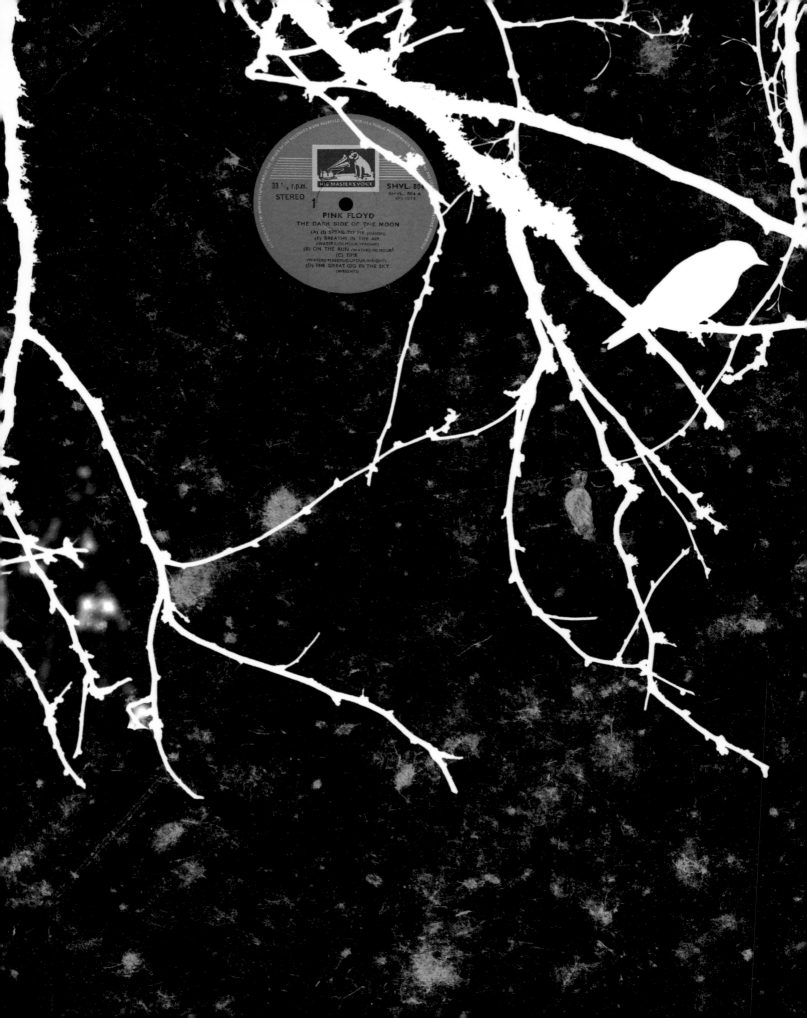

He was glad that someone, that is, I, had turned up.

Apart from which he had taken a liking to me, even
in the darkness, because of my voice, my steps.

Date 196 .	Particulars	Debit (Amt. Withdraw Rs.

'If,' said Victor Halfwit, 'you had not

appeared, I would inevitably have

died a horrible death.

As you know, the most horrible death occurs
when one freezes to death.'

When I said that I was a *doctor*, the man—
whose name, I must admit, most preoccupied me
and not his condition at that moment
(just think, he was called Halfwit!)—

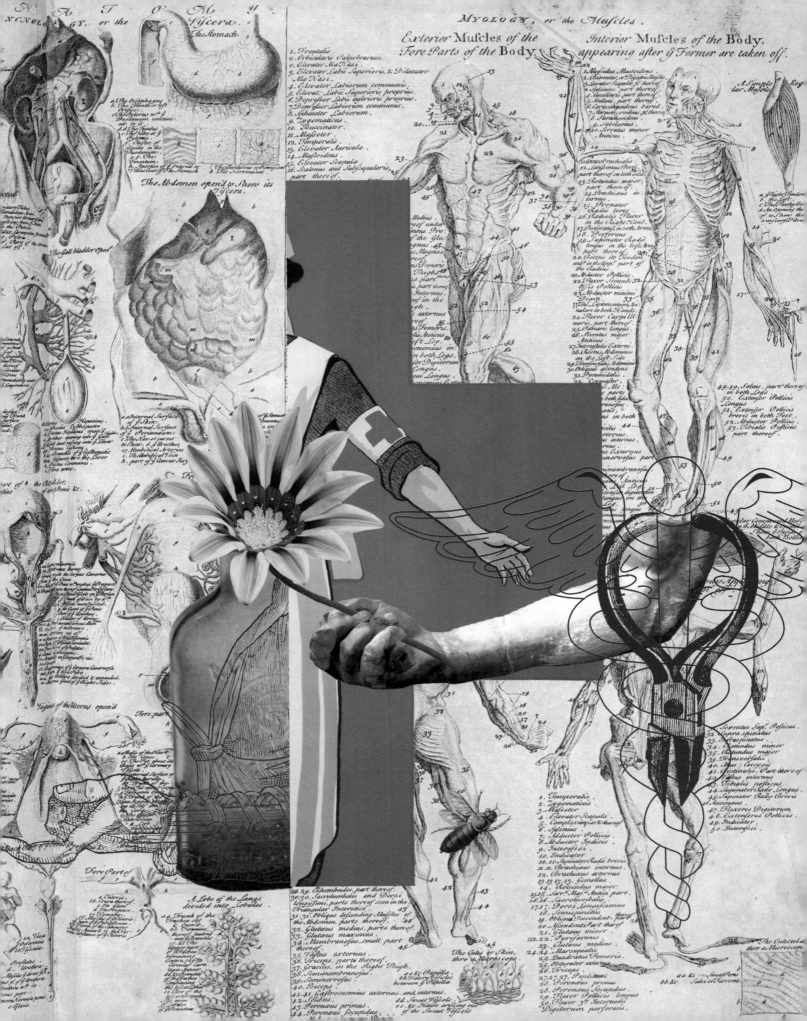

was much happier than if I had said
I was a plumber

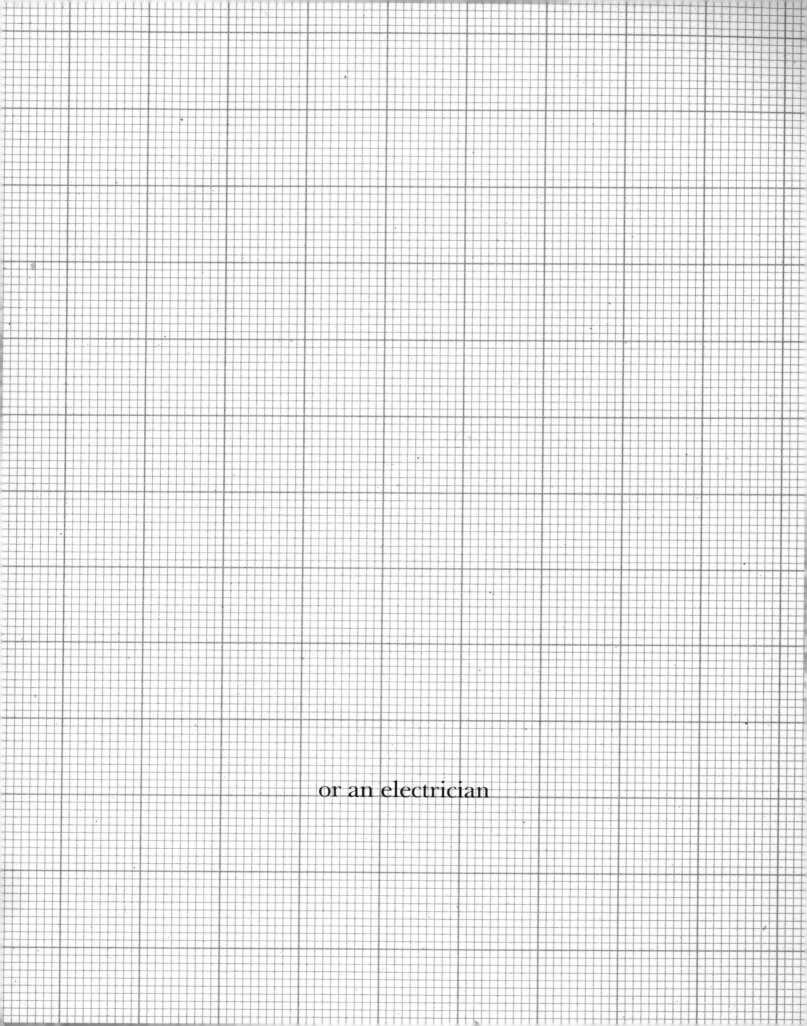

or an electrician

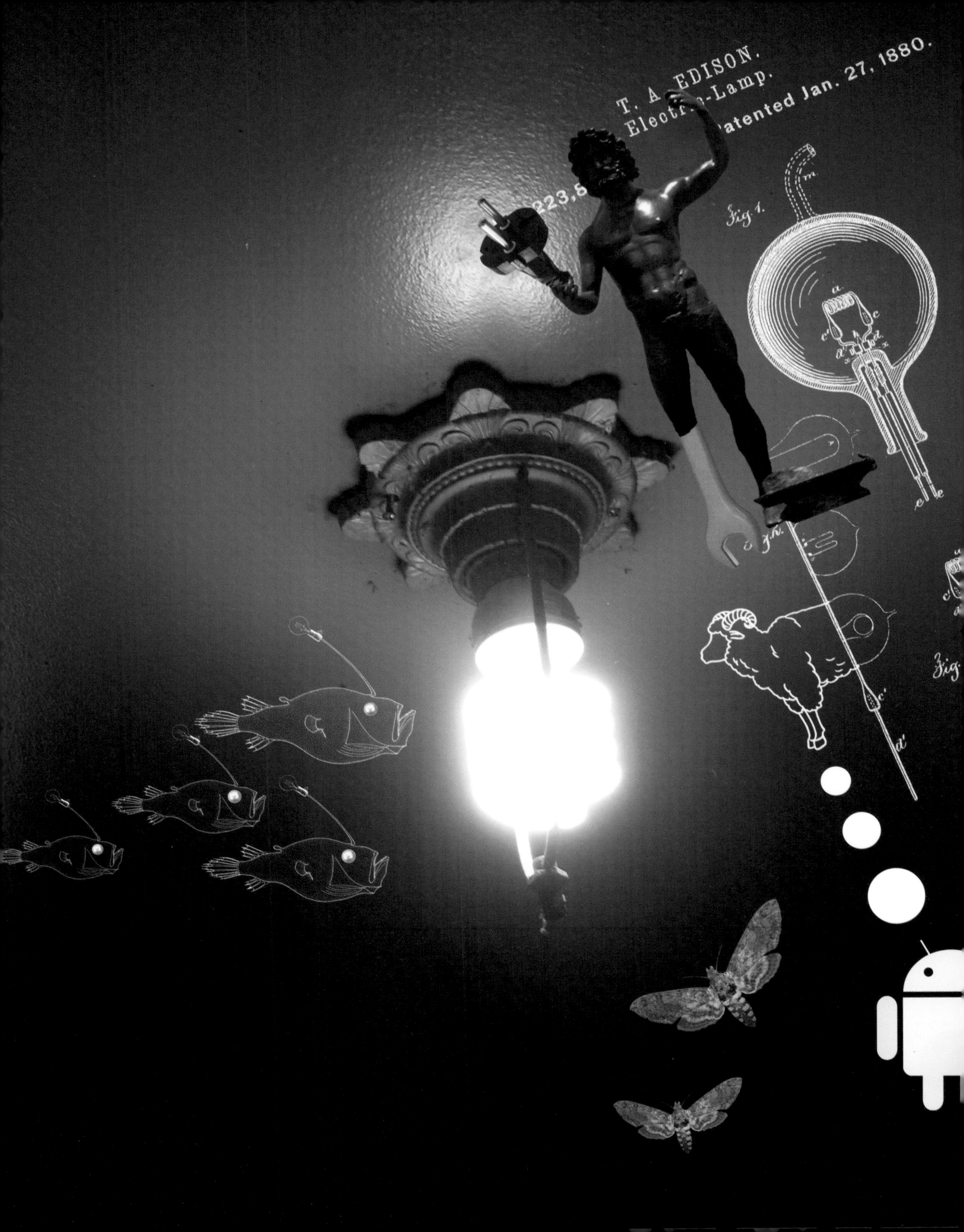
T. A. EDISON.
Electric-Lamp.
Patented Jan. 27, 1880.
Fig. 1.

or a baker

or a farmer.

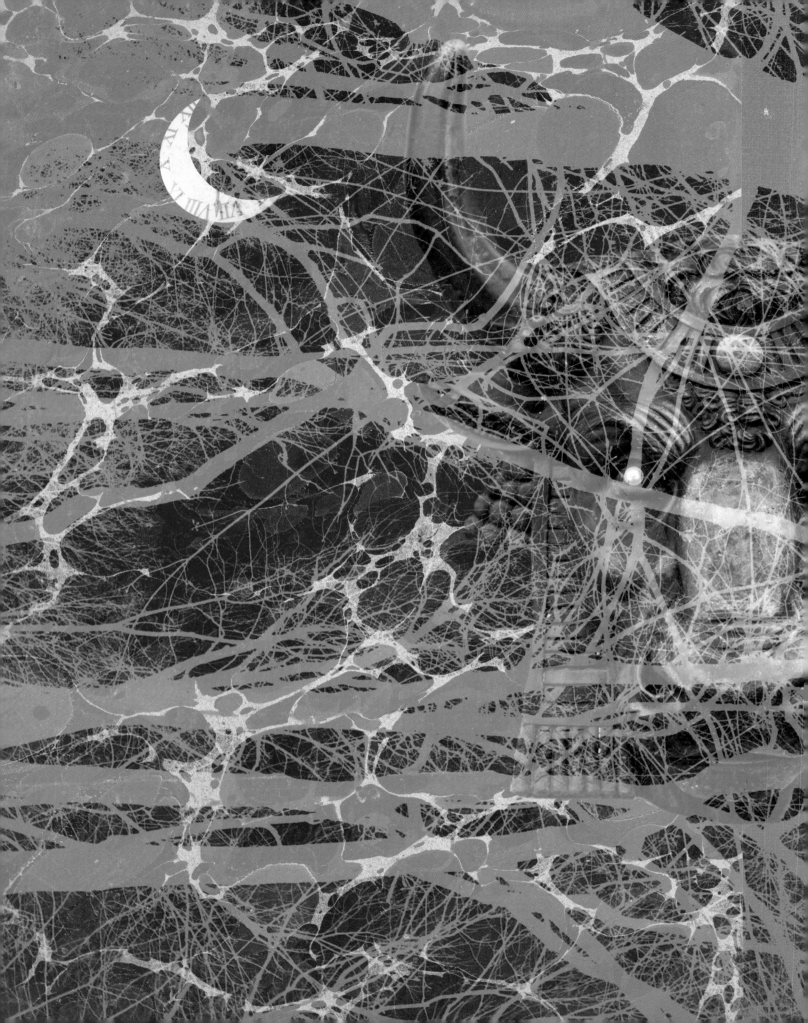

When I asked him how he had ended up in the high forest,
which even for the healthiest could at times be fatal,
and that too between eleven and twelve at night,

he said that he,
and only an hour ago at that,
had made a bet

with a mill-owner from Traich,
whom for years he had only heard about
and not known by sight,
in Traich therefore,
on one side of the high forest.

The mill-owner from Traich
had wagered the sum of eight hundred
schillings

(which is the price of the best pair of Russia
leather boots from our best shoemaker,
which he, Victor Halfwit, has wanted for
more than ten years now),

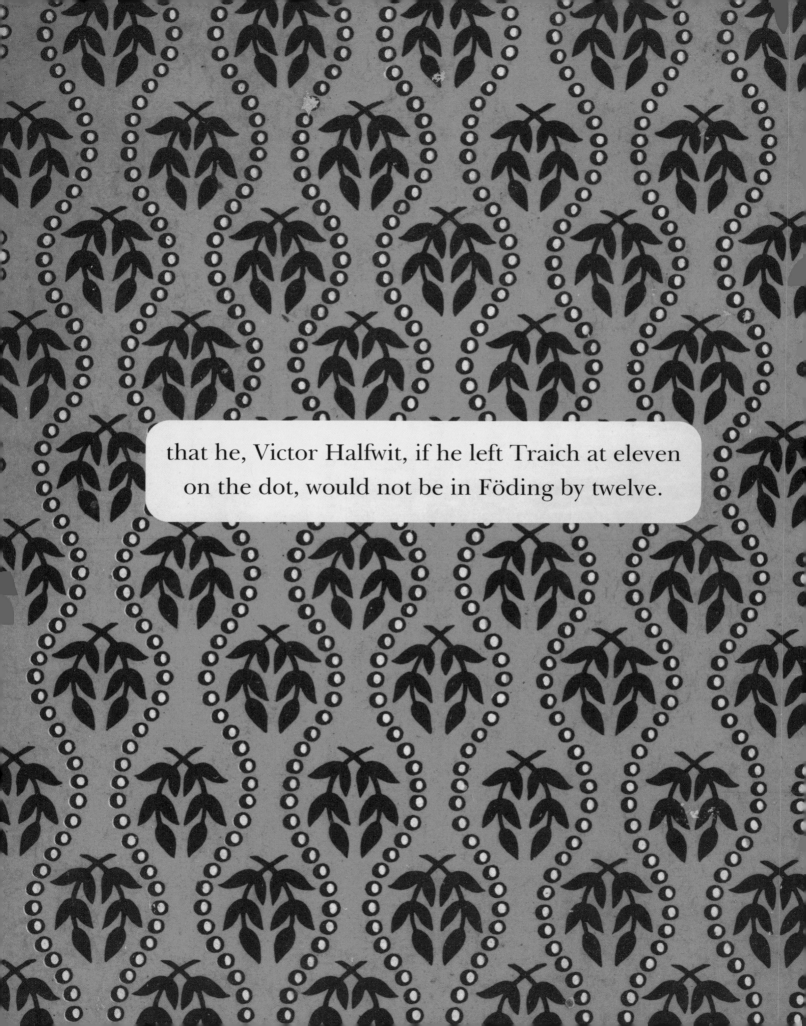

that he, Victor Halfwit, if he left Traich at eleven on the dot, would not be in Föding by twelve.

... velvet smooth action

and that makes you think, naturally, of Activity Board.
smooth, close-textured and brilliant white. Activity is
Board for greeting cards, record sleeves, high class menus
and firm, yet easily fol
Activity is mill conditioned for printability. It will gi
superlative results by any process—particularly by letterpress.
Quality for price, Activity Board has no rival.
Stocked in 2, 3, 3½, 4 and 5 sheet in 20½ × 25 and 22½ × 28½
and readily available from Nash Mills or any of our eleven
Branch Stocks.

SLOW

John Dickinson & Co. Ltd.

He would not make it through the high forest
in an hour on his wooden legs;

not in winter;
not on such a cold night.

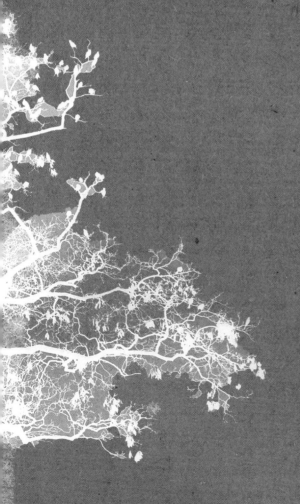

He, Victor Halfwit, had himself not believed he
would be in Föding by twelve.

Nevertheless ('what a fool!'), because one
shouldn't let slip an opportunity which can be
turned to advantage, he had set out from Traich
at eleven as agreed.

The mill-owner had predicted that he would
come to a frightful end, that is,
as already mentioned, by freezing to death.
('How right the mill-owner nearly was!')

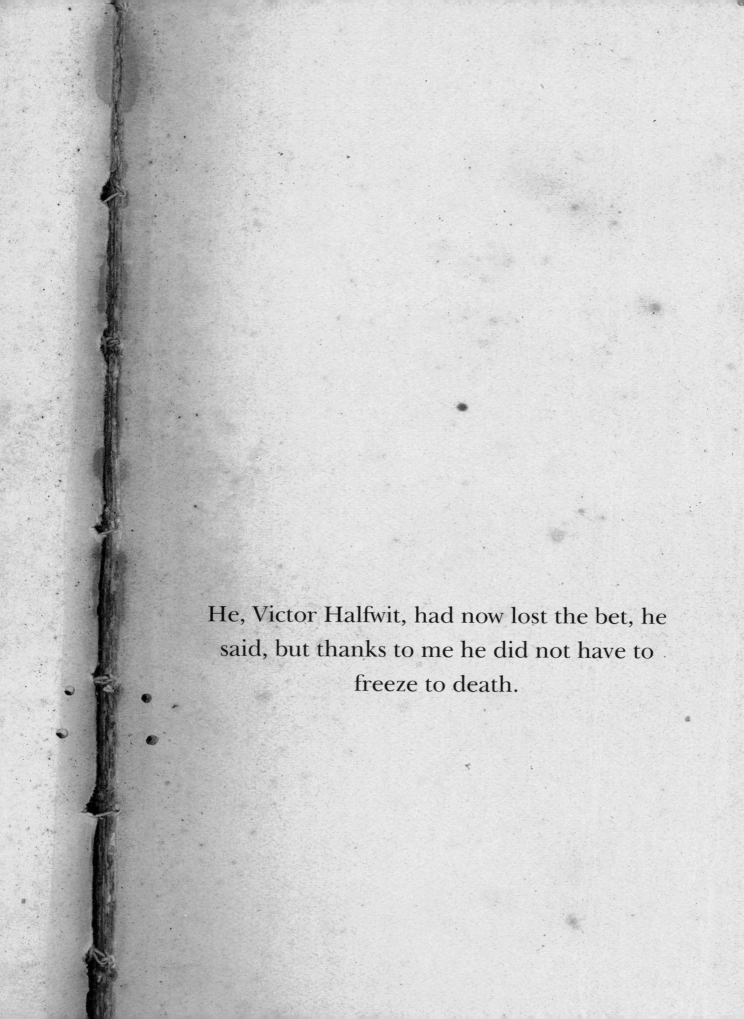

He, Victor Halfwit, had now lost the bet, he
said, but thanks to me he did not have to
freeze to death.

In addition, he had the good fortune
to be rescued from this dreadful situation—which,
he remarked emphatically, like everything in the world
had its ridiculous side—

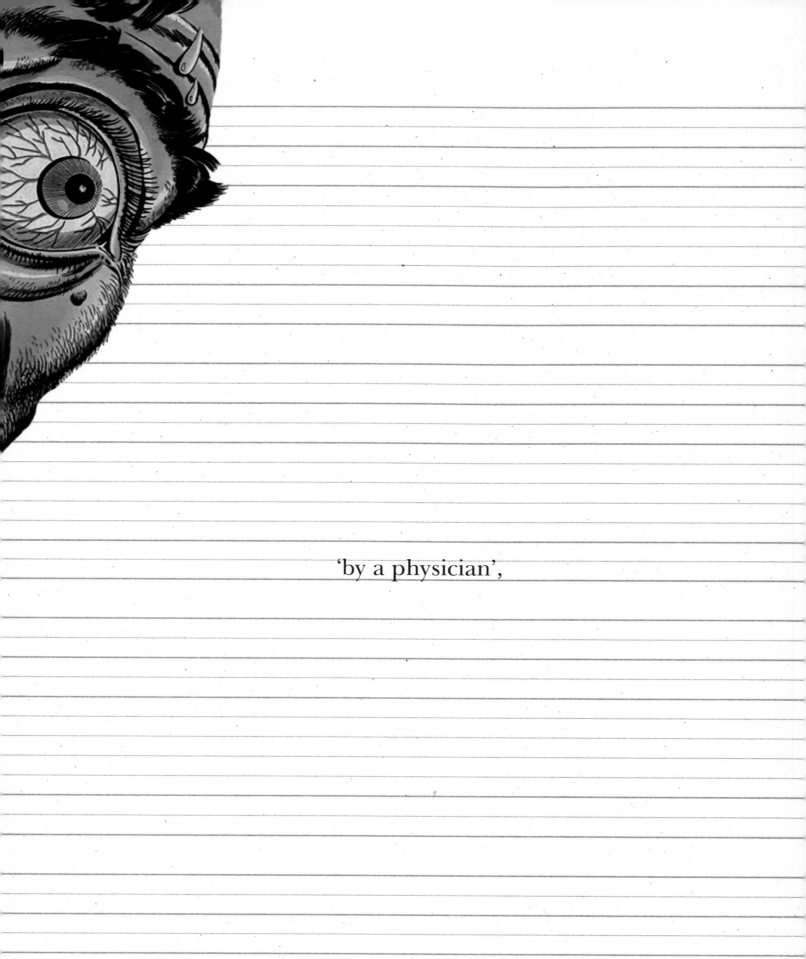

'by a physician',

BRVEGEL INVEN 1557

Fig. 6.

by a *proper* doctor.

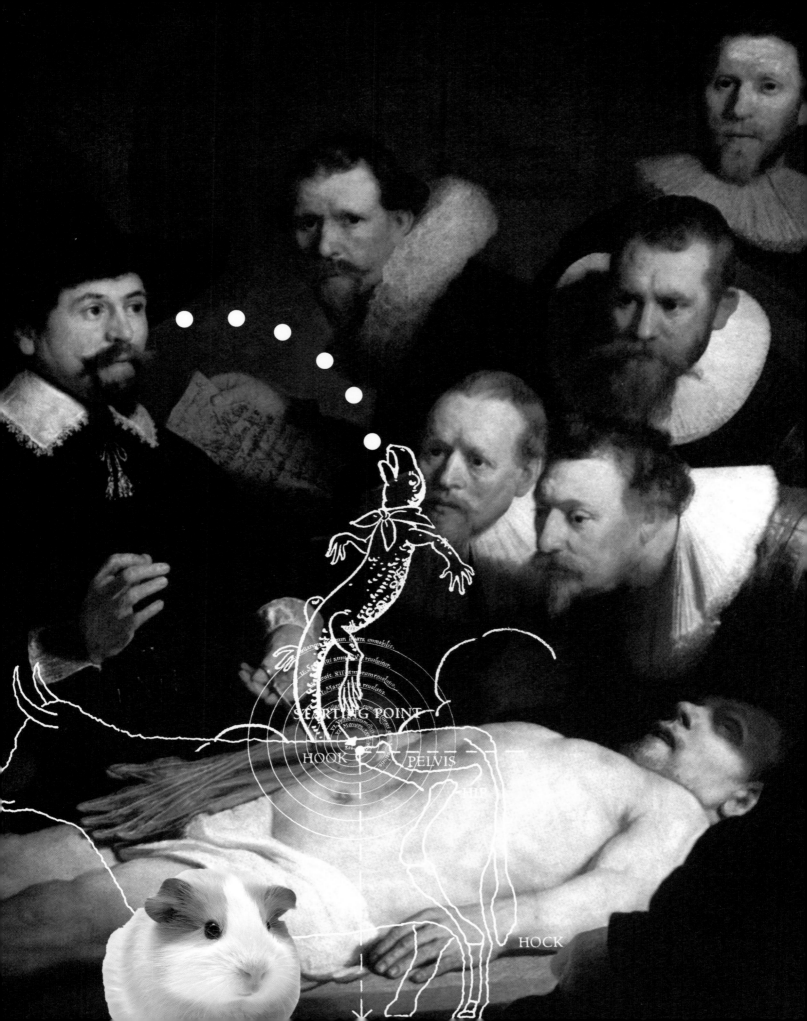

STARTING POINT

HOOK   PELVIS

HIP

HOCK

I sat him up
and brushed most of the
snow off him

and established that both his wooden
legs really had snapped in the middle,
as wooden legs do.

Without a moment's hesitation,
because I had to get to my patient as quickly as possible,
I lifted him onto my shoulders.

It would have been better
if I had been able to carry him
without the wooden legs,

but neither of us could undo the buckles
which were frozen solid.

The broken wooden legs were frozen to his thighs, and I thought the man must be in terrible pain

as well as weakened by
his fear of approaching death.

But because such a person
is used to great pain

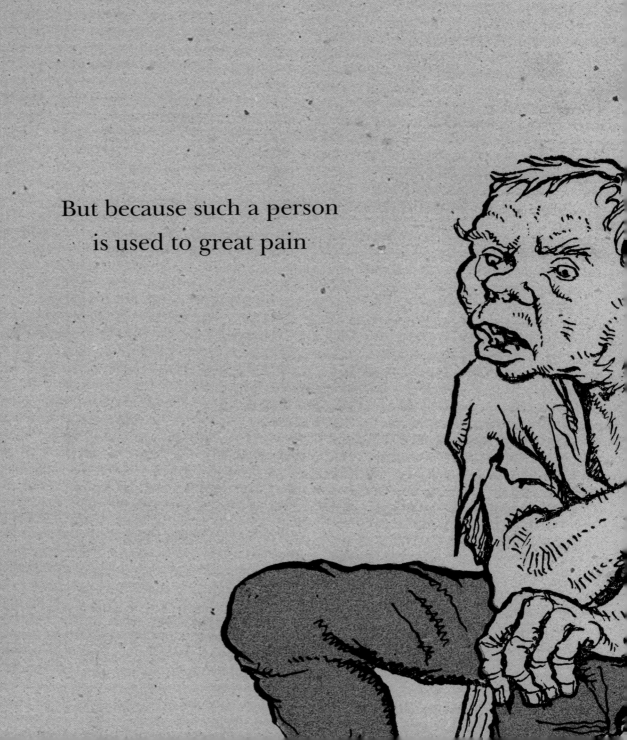

(one is used to it, if one no longer has any legs, none
of one's own, legs of bone and flesh and blood,

if one only has artificial ones)

he didn't wail,

he didn't blubb,

he didn't cry out,
he didn't complain at all.

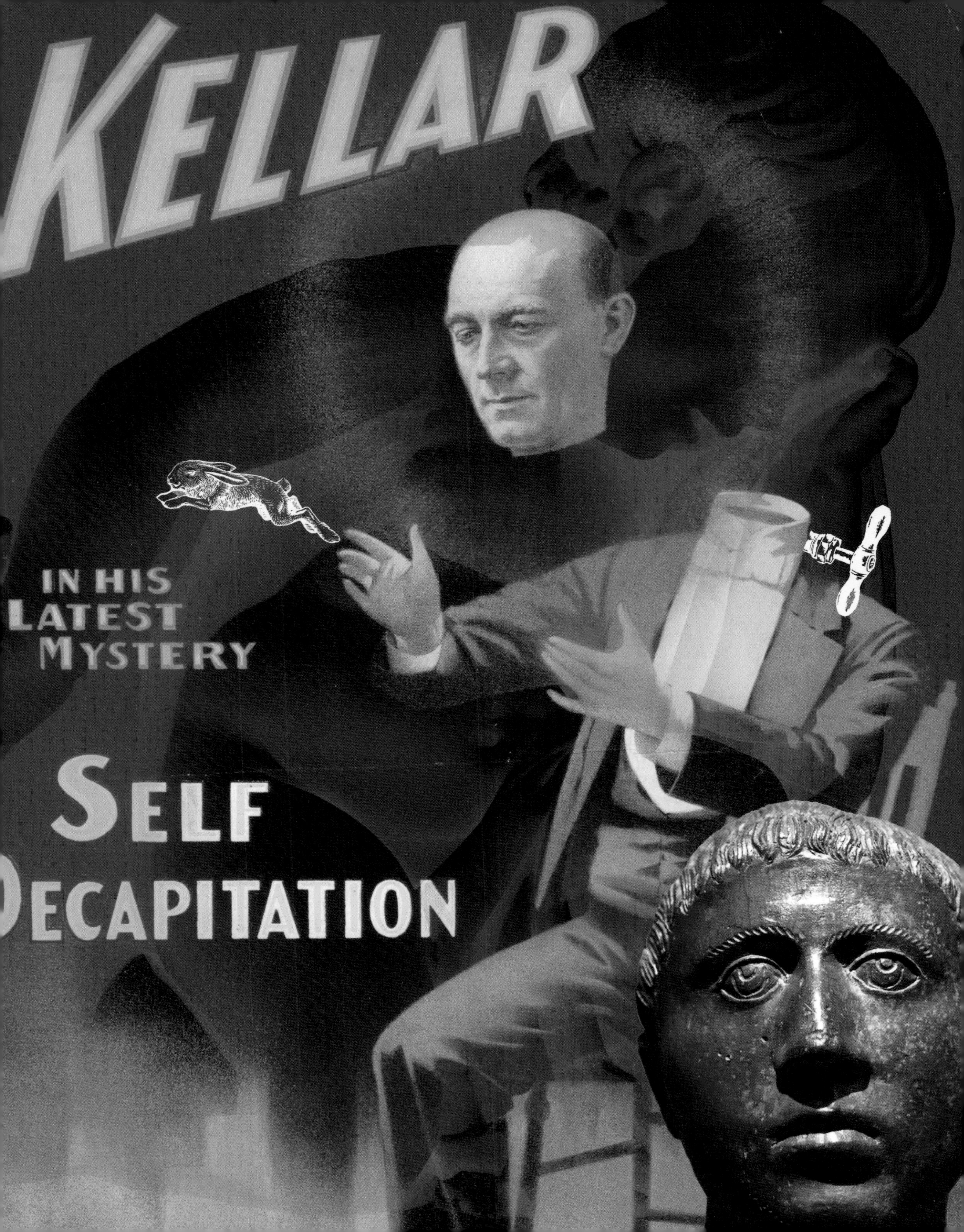
KELLAR
IN HIS
LATEST
MYSTERY
SELF
DECAPITATION

We saw that in 1802 it gave a reward to Gr— In 1807, it awarded a gold medal to Christopher of London, for a "neutral-built, self-balanced The sides of this boat had outer and inner with an air space between." Wilson, like L— tended that his system should be followed in struction of "all open boats of whatever form but a boat to his design had been specially built a— at Newhaven, in competition with one of Gr— Life-Boats, and apparently it was her excellent b— in a heavy sea which won for Wilson the rewa— gold medal.

The Society gave three other rewards, in 18— and 1817 respectively. The first was one of 20 and the silver medal to Mr. Bremner, Minister and Flota, in the Orkneys, for his plan of co— any ship's boat into a Life-Boat by means of em— lashed inside the boat, one forward and the o— and packed in with bundles of cork covered w— operation being completed by the attachm— of iron or lead to the inside of the ke— was one of 10 guineas, and the silver — —re, of Dean-street, Fetter-lane, for an — — be held suspended at the stern of a — —d if a man fell overboard. It carried a — —nch, if set up, would enable it, so Mr. B— to follow a ship or reach the shore. The thir— silver medal to Captain Gabriel Bray, for hi— making ordinary boats buoyant by means o— air-boxes to be fastened by copper clasps t— thwarts, and long air-cases to be lashed fore outside. The inventions were no doubt pre— good faith as original, and they were certainly — but they were not novel in principle; and it — to restrain a smile at the details of two of them

No, on the contrary,
he was glad to be rescued

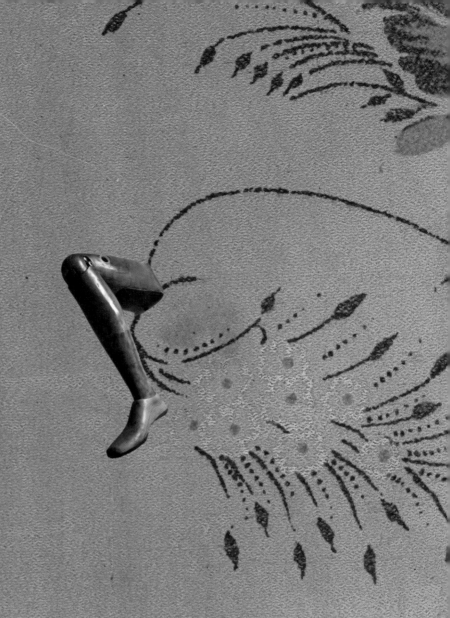

so I shouldered him
and firmly gripped the wooden legs,
crossed them and held them to my chest,

so not only doubling, as it seemed to me,
the weight which I had to carry, but multiplying
it three times, five times, fourteen times,

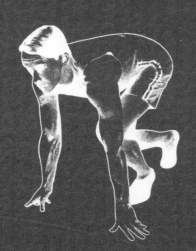

in order to advance as swiftly as possible
out of the high forest to Föding.

It didn't occur to Victor Halfwit
that he would be in Föding before twelve

and so win the bet with the mill-owner

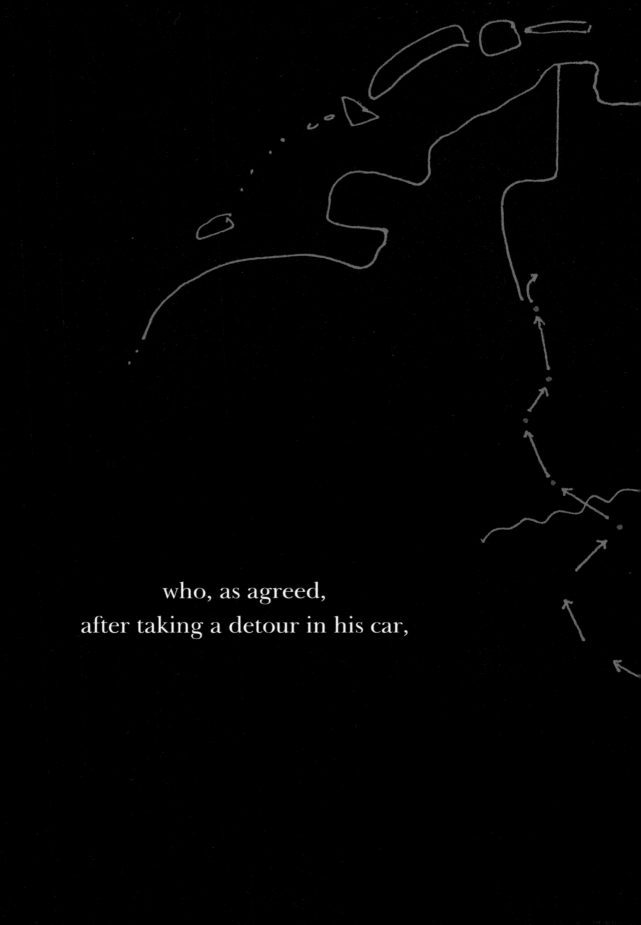

who, as agreed,
after taking a detour in his car,

was already waiting
at the place.

He didn't even think such a thing,
but I suddenly had the feeling,
after glancing at my watch
at exactly half past eleven

the result of
may be com-
Others again
(*see* Herod.
various the
—an expan-
in the narrow
for popula-
of Greek
the Roman
nations in the
are distin-
cant that the
in a position
it formed a
political sub-
was com-
ited a co
; the po
es esta
s of i
thenia
and a
proper
ercial or se
e her colony
out the revolt
it is not ea
(*e.g.*, the rela-
sian Wars, to
). When we
dern colonies
as even more
of colour and
colonization
Greek settle-
d themselves
here the na-
e of a stock
rated from it
th the native
or intellectual
th which the
the highest in
in the Great
blood in their
e absence of
isted between
f the colonial
ion[1], nor was

that I, and so on my back also Victor Halfwit,
could be in Föding by twelve

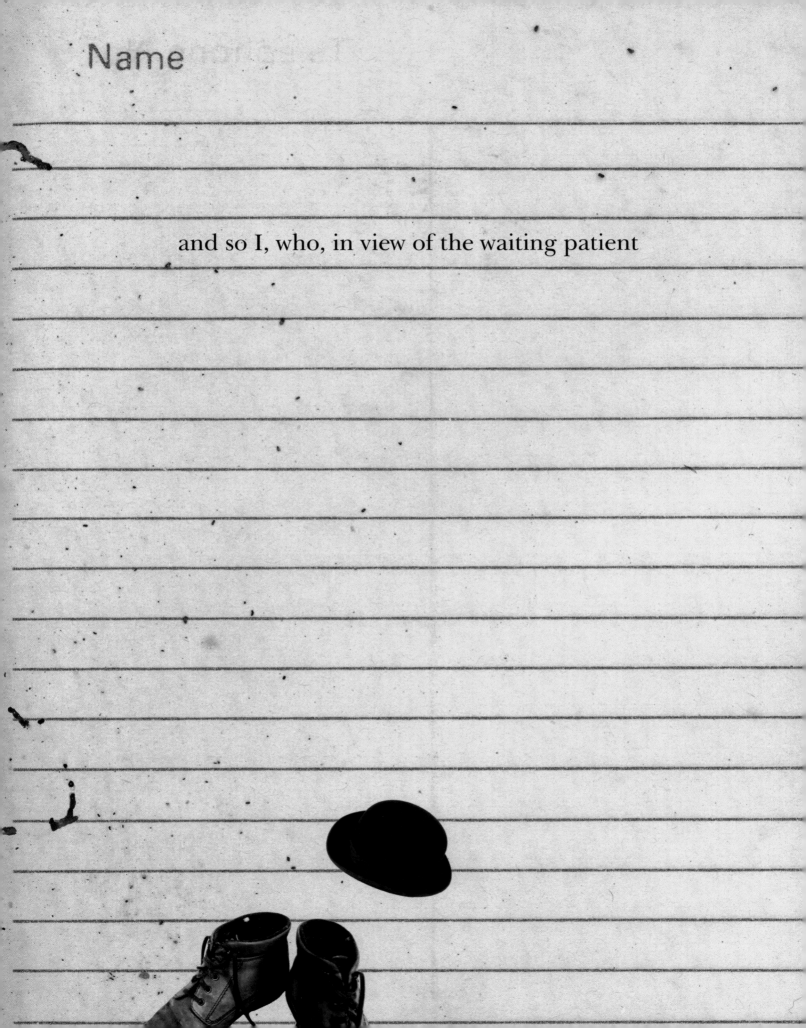

Name

and so I, who, in view of the waiting patient

had already been running
quite fast through the high forest

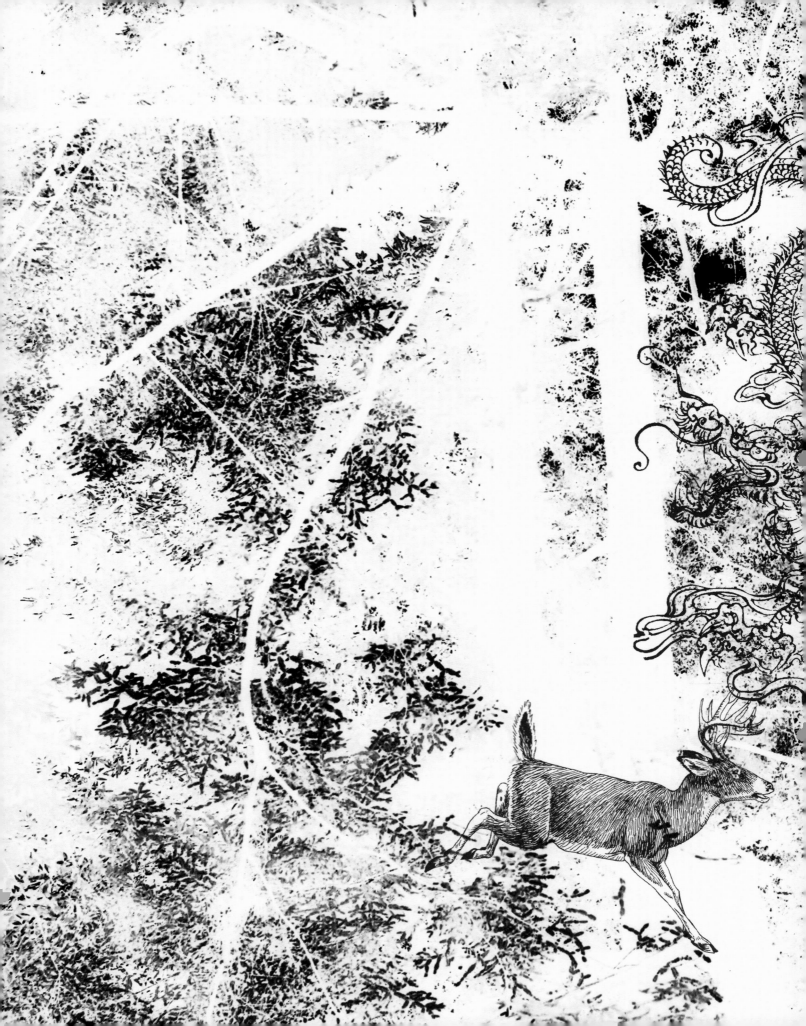

began
to run
even faster
through the high
forest

with the man on my back,
who was rather fat and soft

and who, out of fear at my pace,
didn't dare say another word.

Not until we had left the
high forest behind,

shortly before the lights of Föding,
did he say, 'Is that not Föding?'

and I replied, 'Yes, Föding, indeed, Föding!'

And then he asked
whether it was already twelve.
To which I answered,
'No, it has not struck twelve,

not yet.'

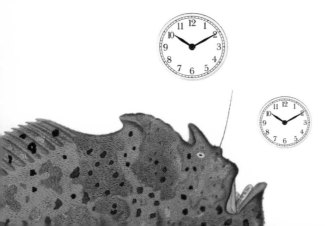

As I ran, as if I had lost my senses,

Victor Halfwit said that he had agreed
to meet the mill-owner not simply in Föding
but 'at the *church door* in Föding'.

'At the *church door*! That's a stroke of luck,' I said, 'because my patient is waiting for me nearby.'

And as I ran I managed to say,
just as we arrived at the church square,
'It isn't twelve yet!'

Lucy

and I dashed to the church door
and truly a man was standing in front of it,
tall, dark,

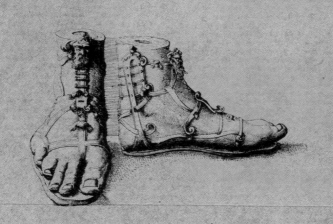

and I thought,
'You'll now throw Victor Halfwit at his feet
but in such a way that the fall doesn't hurt him.'

I did so,

and the bell struck twelve.

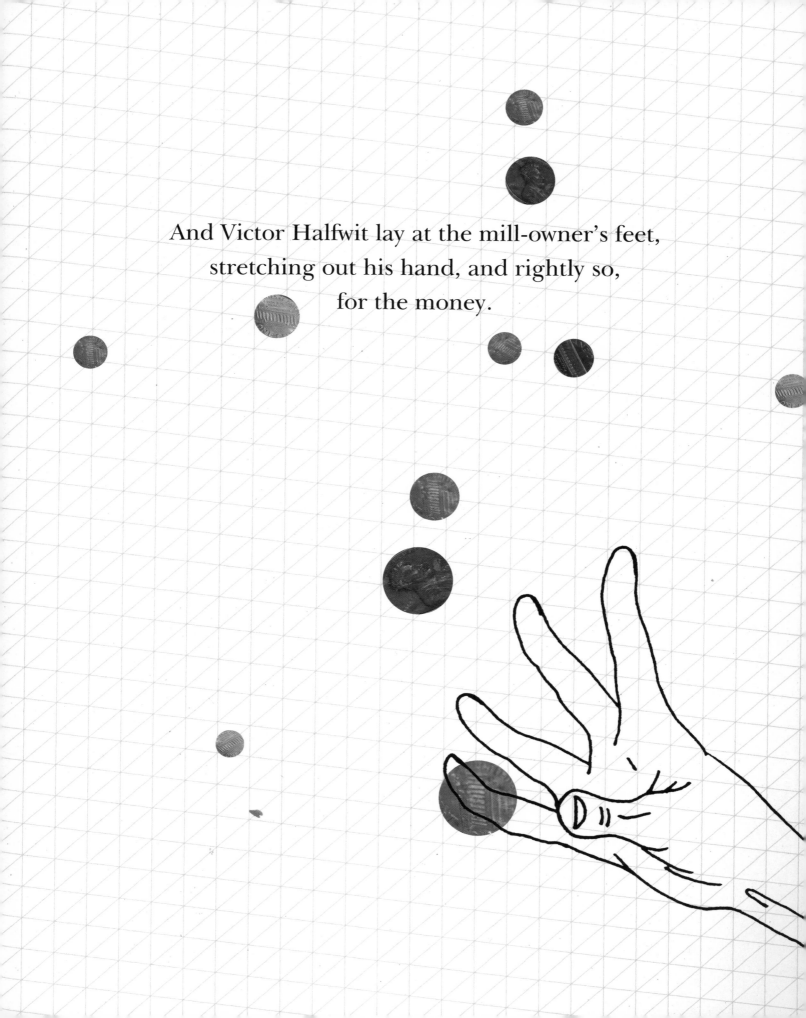

And Victor Halfwit lay at the mill-owner's feet,
stretching out his hand, and rightly so,
for the money.

Altogether astonished by the whole thing,
but finally, after I had introduced myself and
addressed him sharply, the tall, dark mill-owner
pulled out his big, black wallet,

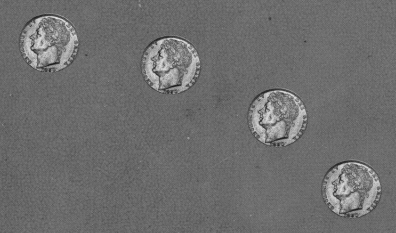

more because he was afraid, less because he
accepted that he had lost the bet, and counted out
eight one hundred schilling notes into Victor
Halfwit's hand, who was still lying on the ground.

'A bet is a bet,' said the mill-owner, who had not anticipated the possibility that someone might pick Victor Halfwit up in the middle of the high forest and run to Föding with him.

THE LIVING WORLD

ILLUSTRATED

He would not, said the mill-owner, have given
a farthing for Victor Halfwit's life.

He was surprised that anyone could enter
into such a wager at all!

'I already saw Victor Halfwit dead!'
said the mill-owner

and then, 'Oh well, *doctors*!
Really, doctors stick their noses into everything!'

and he disappeared.

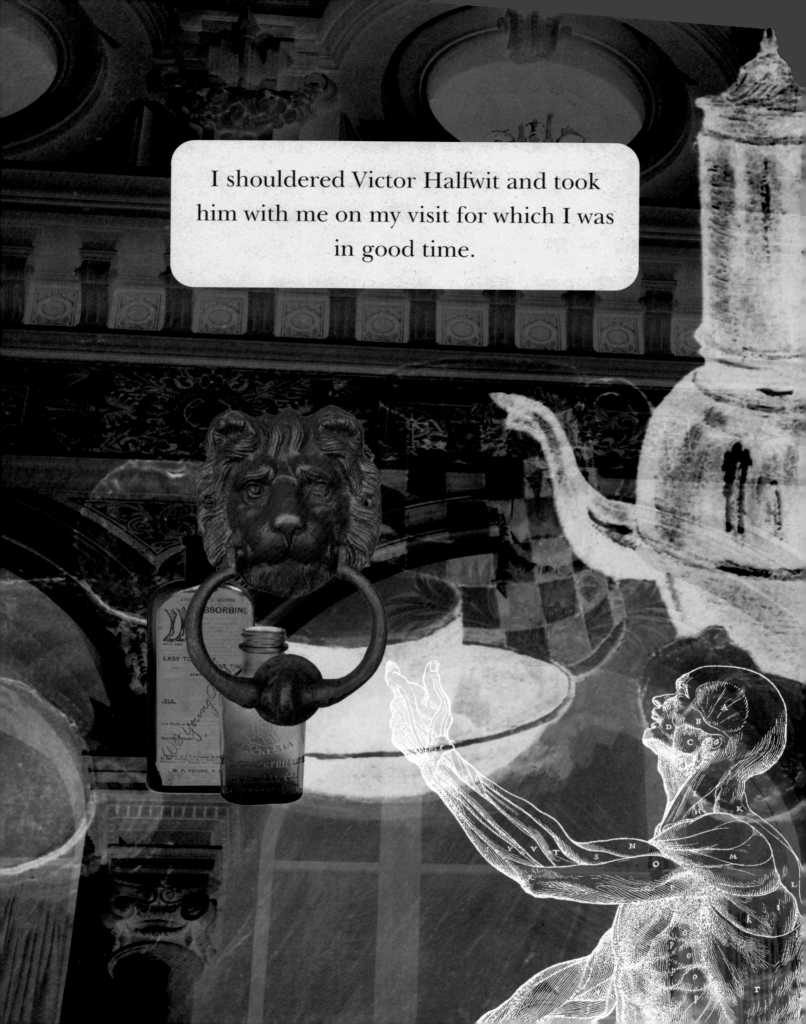

I shouldered Victor Halfwit and took him with me on my visit for which I was in good time.

Afterwards, I requested a bed for the night in the nearby inn for Victor Halfwit and paid for it in advance.

We came to an agreement not to concern ourselves any further with each other.

Curiously enough, Victor Halfwit took advantage of our leavetaking to thank me.

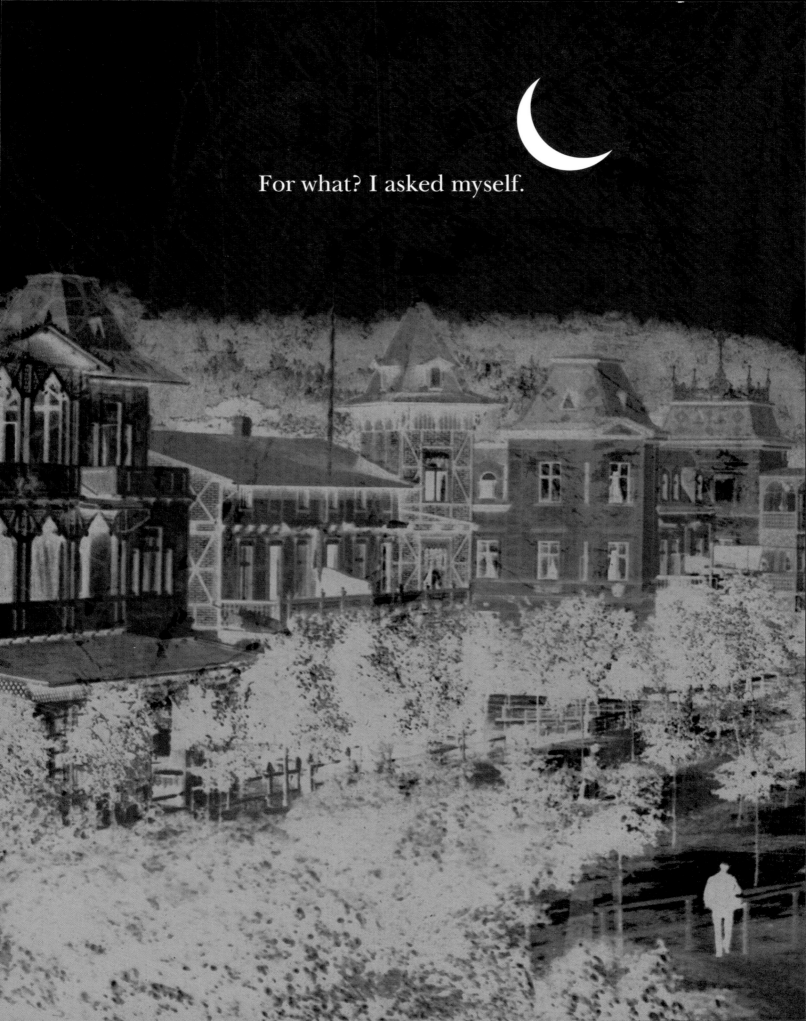

For what? I asked myself.

And on the way home,

I thought that although he had won the bet,

that is, eight hundred schillings for a pair
of the best Russia leather boots from our
best shoemaker,

THE COMEDY DRAMA
THE SHOEMAKER

A PLAY FULL OF TEARS AN LAUGHTER

he had lost his wooden legs.

And those will cost him two and a half thousand.

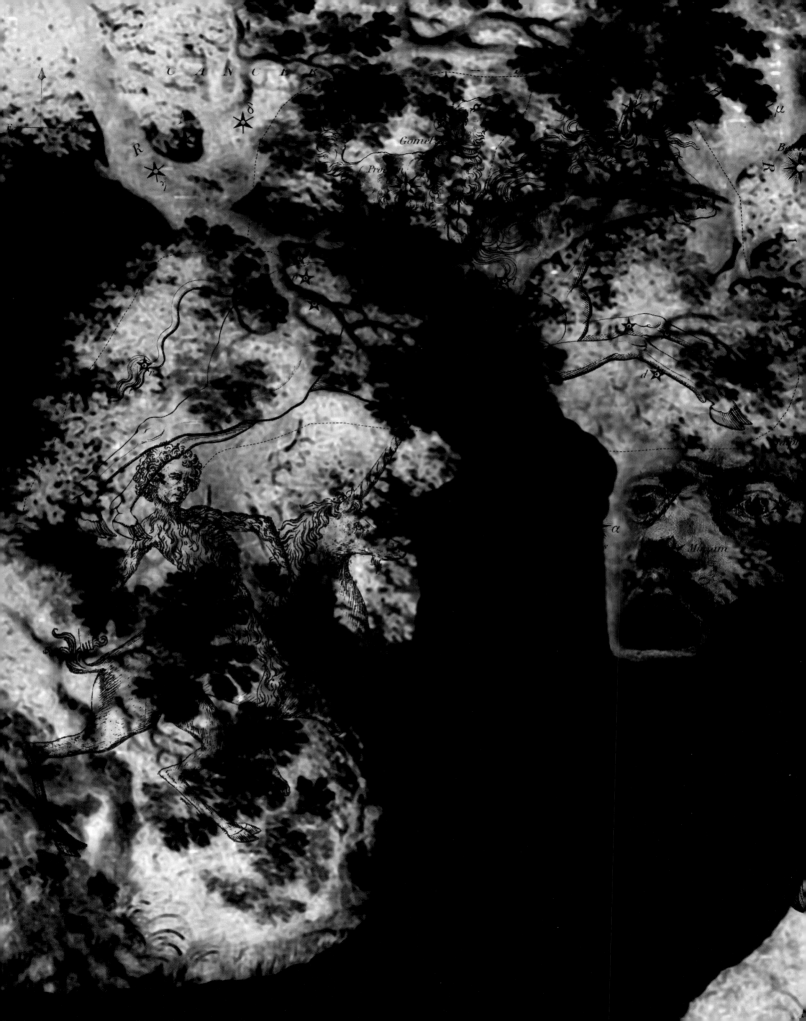

What kind of a man, I thought in the high forest, who plagued me so greatly on my walk that I thought I must die, is Victor Halfwit?

Is he crazy?

GOETHE-INSTITUT

This publication was supported by
a grant from the Goethe-Institut India

Seagull Books 2011

Thomas Bernhard, *Viktor Halbnarr. Ein Wintermärchen*, from Thomas Bernhard, *Erzählungen.*
Kurzprosa. Herausgegeben von Hans Höller, Martin Huber und Manfred Mittermayer (= Thomas
Bernhard, *Werke. Herausgegeben von Martin Huber und Wendelin Schmidt-Dengler. Band 14*)
© Suhrkamp Verlag, Frankfurt am Main, 2003.

First published in English by Seagull Books, 2011

English translation © Martin Chalmers 2011
Digital collages © Sunandini Banerjee 2011

Seagull Books is grateful to Chandana Hore for the use of her own
and Somnath Hore's works.

ISBN-13   978 1 9064 9 764 4

British Library Cataloguing-in-Publication Data
A catalogue record for this book is available
from the British Library

Printed and bound in Calcutta, India, at CDC Printers